CONTENTS

Words that look like this are hockey lingo. Learn more about them on page 8.
Words that look like THIS are explained in the glossary on page 31.

THE BASICS

TEAM HUDDLE

So, you want to play field hockey? This book will teach you all about what to say, what to wear, and how to play. From learning the lingo to earning a place in the Hall of Fame, this book will give you the know-how!

GRAB YOUR FRIENDS AND SHIN PADS – IT'S TIME TO PLAY!

Field hockey is a game played by two teams; each team can have 11 players on the **pitch** at any one time. The players use field hockey sticks to hit, push, and **dribble** a ball to try to get it in the OPPOSING team's goal.

Field hockey is a very fast-paced game that is full of strategy. What does strategy mean? In sports, a strategy is when you have made a plan of how to score before playing the game. Field hockey players have to be able to think and act quickly to make sure the strategies work.

NOT EVERYTHING GOES AS PLANNED, AND PLAYERS HAVE TO BE ABLE TO QUICKLY CHANGE THEIR PLANS TO WIN.

Field hockey is a noncontact sport. This means that players aren't allowed to push or bump into other players on purpose. However, because of how fast the game is played, players sometimes bump into each other accidentally. The sticks can also be dangerous; it is important to wear shin pads to protect your legs.

TYPES OF HOCKEY

FIELD HOCKEY

Field hockey refers to a popular type of hockey that is played on real or SYNTHETIC grass and is played outside. Indoor hockey is another variation of field hockey that is played, as the name suggests, inside.

IF YOUR PITCH IS FROZEN, YOU MAY AS WELL BE PLAYING ICE HOCKEY!

ICE HOCKEY

Ice hockey is similar to field hockey, except that players don't run on the ground. Instead they skate on ice and use a puck instead of a ball. This type of hockey is even quicker, with more protective gear and collisions!

ICE HOCKEY IS A POPULAR SPORT IN CANADA AND PARTS OF THE UNITED STATES.

UNDERWATER HOCKEY

As the name suggests, this type of hockey is played underwater. Players try to stay underwater as long as possible or risk losing control of the puck. This sport is very hard and demanding on the lungs. How long can you hold your breath?

Sometimes underwater hockey is called "octopush."

POWER HOCKEY

Power hockey is a type of hockey that has been adapted for people with disabilities. Players use wheelchairs to move around the pitch. Other than that, the game is very similar to indoor field hockey.

POWER HOCKEY TEAM

THE LINGO

The lingo, the slang, the vocab. Whatever you call it, learning the words behind specific sports can be a very daunting task! Here are some of the strangest and weirdest words that will help you talk the field hockey talk in no time.

DRIBBLE

Moving the ball around the pitch and away from defenders by using short, skillful taps to keep the ball in your possession.

ATTACKING

When a team is trying to score a goal.

DEFENSIVE

A way you can organize your team and playing style to make it harder for the opponents to get to your goal. Instead of focusing on attacking, your team places importance on defending.

TACKLE

To regain possession of the ball from an opponent by using your stick to pull the ball away or block a pass between two players.

FREE HIT

A hit, or shot, that is given to the opposing team if you commit a foul outside the shooting circle.

OFFENSIVE

A way you can organize your team and playing style to make it more likely that you will score. Instead of focusing on defending, your team places importance on attacking.

PITCH

The pitch, or field, is the area on which the game is played.

PENALTY STROKE

A stroke that is awarded when a serious and deliberate foul takes place in the shooting circle. The game is stopped and a shot on goal is awarded to the attacking team. Only one player from the attacking team and the goalkeeper from the defending team take part in the penalty stroke.

FIND OUT MORE ABOUT THE LAYOUT OF THE PITCH ON PAGE 18.

PENALTY CORNER

A stroke that is awarded when an offense is committed by a defender between the 25-yard line closest to their goal and their back-line. Five defenders including the goalkeeper try and protect the goal from the attacking team. The ball must be passed outside of the shooting circle before being able to shoot.

THE PLAYERS

There are 11 different players on the pitch at any one time in field hockey. The players can be grouped into four different sections: forwards, midfielders, defenders, and goalkeepers.

FORWARDS

Forwards are also known as the offense. They have the responsibility of attacking, which means making accurate shots and scoring goals. Forwards have to be able to SPRINT past the defenders on the opposing team and work together to be able to score goals.

MIDFIELDERS

Midfielders are some of the most VERSATILE players on the field. This is because they have to play between the forwards and defenders. Midfielders also have to be very physically fit because they are constantly running between both ends of the field.

DEFENDERS

Defenders have some of the most important jobs in the game. They have to make sure that players attacking their goal don't succeed. They have to be able to predict what type of shots the opposing team will make and tackle them to stop this from happening.

GOALKEEPERS

Unlike the field players, goalies can use any part of their body, such as their hands and their feet, to stop the ball from going into the goal. Goalies have to stay very calm in the face of attackers and have fast REFLEXES to be able to stop as many goals as possible.

FORMATIONS

A FORMATION IS A TYPE OF PATTERN THE PLAYERS STAND IN WHEN ON THE PITCH. YOU CAN USE DIFFERENT FORMATIONS TO PLAY DIFFERENT TYPES OF GAMES.

For example, if your team knew they were playing a team that was very defensive, your team could play in an offensive formation. This way your team would have a better chance of breaking through their defense and scoring a goal.

On page 13, the players in red are positioned in an offensive way. There are more players in the forward positions than any other section. There are fewer defenders. This way, the team will have a better chance of scoring a goal, but will have a weaker defense.

The players in blue are in a defensive formation. The midfielders and defenders both have four players in their sections and there are only two attackers. This formation will have a better chance of stopping the attackers from scoring a goal, but a smaller chance of scoring themselves.

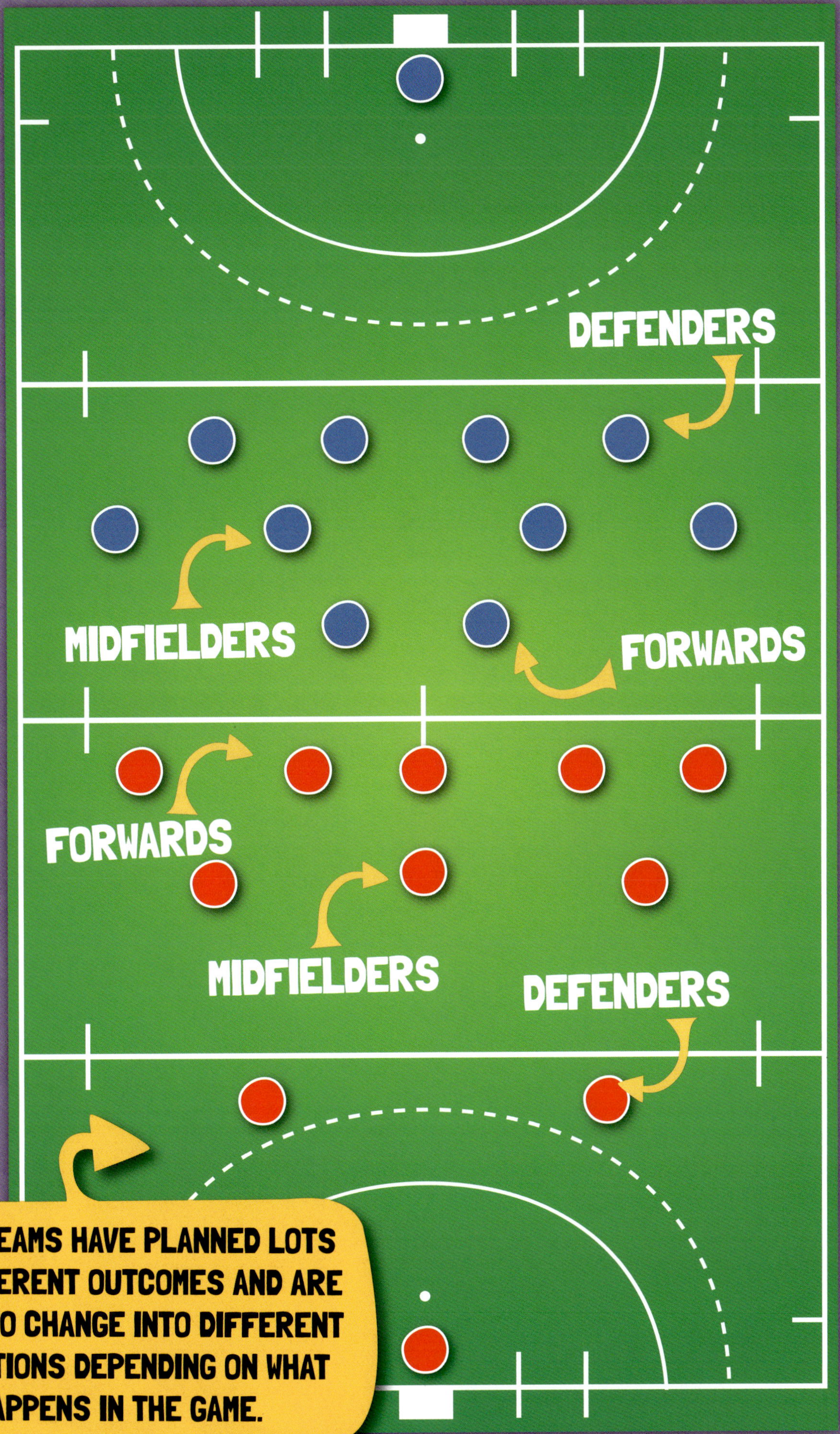

SOME TEAMS HAVE PLANNED LOTS OF DIFFERENT OUTCOMES AND ARE READY TO CHANGE INTO DIFFERENT FORMATIONS DEPENDING ON WHAT HAPPENS IN THE GAME.

THE UNIFORM

Field hockey is a fast-paced sport that is a very good form of exercise, with lots of running up and down the field. It can also be quite dangerous with the sticks and a ball flying in all directions. This is why it is important to make sure you are wearing the correct protective clothing.

A field hockey player's outfit usually consists of a sleeveless top made out of stretchy, **BREATHABLE** fabric. On the bottom, players can often choose to wear either shorts, leggings, or a skirt. These also have to be stretchy so that players can easily move around.

SOME PLAYERS CHOOSE TO WEAR GLOVES TO IMPROVE THEIR GRIP.

What footwear you choose will depend on what kind of surface you are playing on. If you are playing on real turf, you need to wear shoes with cleats so that you don't slip and fall. Cleats dig into the ground when you're running and stop you from slipping.

CLEATS

CLEATS AREN'T ALLOWED ON SYNTHETIC TURF, SO NORMAL SNEAKERS ARE USED INSTEAD.

Goalkeepers need to wear more protective gear because they are at a higher risk of getting hit by the ball. Some of their protective clothing includes: padded gloves, leg protectors, feet pads, padded shorts, and chest and throat pads. They also wear a different color shirt than the rest of their team.

ALL THIS PROTECTION IS NEEDED BECAUSE FIELD HOCKEY BALLS CAN TRAVEL AT AROUND 60 MILES (100 KM) PER HOUR!

THE EQUIPMENT

THE BALL

Field hockey balls are a standardized object in the sport. The ball must be between 8.8 inches and 9.3 inches (22.4 and 23.5 cm) in CIRCUMFERENCE and must weigh between 5.5 ounces and 5.7 ounces (156 and 163 g).

Other players also need protective equipment that is an ESSENTIAL part of their gear. Some of these things include a mouth guard and shin pads. A mouth guard is to protect your teeth in case the ball accidentally hits you in the face. The shin pads are to protect your legs from the sticks and ball accidentally hitting and bruising your legs.

Standardized objects make the sport fair by making sure every game is played with the same type of equipment.

SHIN PADS

MOUTH GUARD

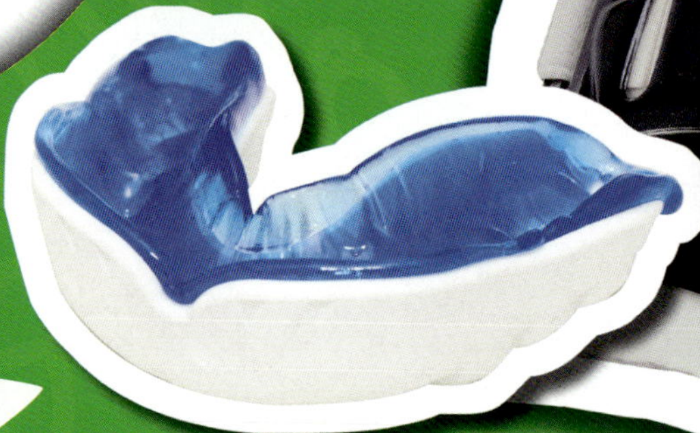

THE STICK

Field hockey sticks are two sided; one side is flat and the other is curved. The flat side is the playing side and the curved side is the nonplaying side. A rule in field hockey is that the stick cannot weigh more than 1.6 pounds (737 g).

LARGER HEADS WITH MORE SURFACE AREA CAN HELP YOU TO CONTROL THE BALL, BUT SMALLER HEADS ARE GOOD FOR MOVING QUICKLY WITH THE BALL.

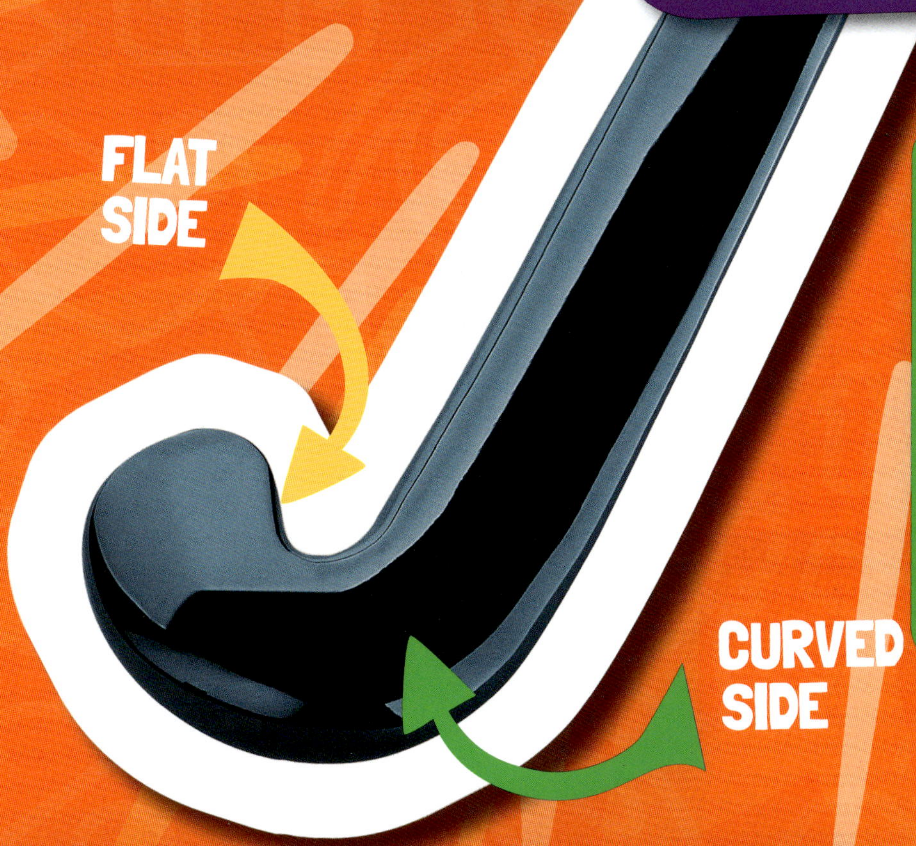

There are lots of different types of sticks and it's important to get the right stick for you and the position you play. Often, defenders play with heavier sticks and forwards play with lighter sticks. There are also sticks with differently shaped heads.

THE PITCH

back-line
60 yards
11 yards
STRIKING CIRCLE
A circular shape marked in front of each goal. To score a goal, the ball must be hit from inside this area.
PENALTY SPOT
The point at which a penalty stroke is taken from.
25-YARD LINES
Two lines that, with the center line, split the pitch into four equal quarters.

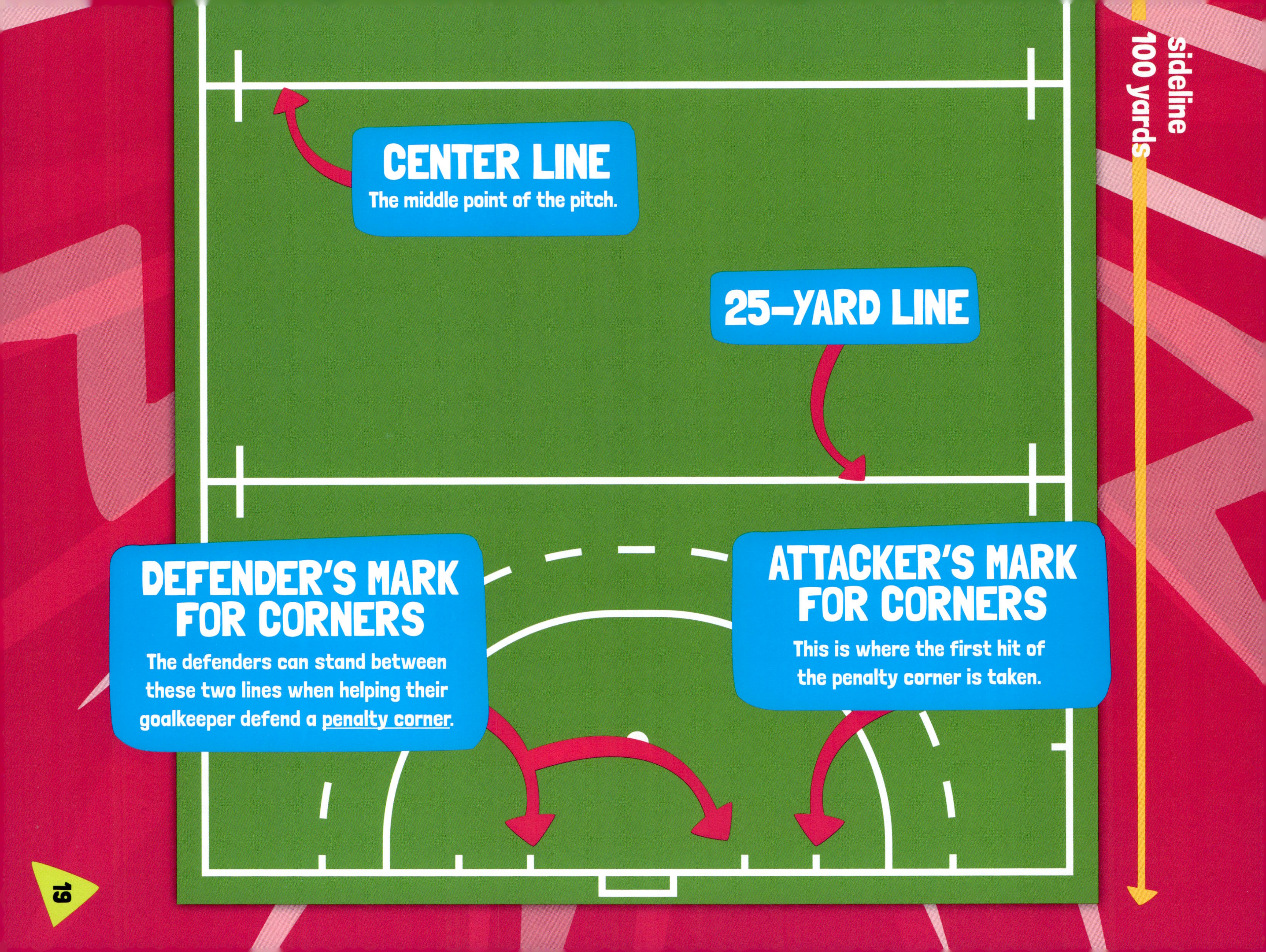
sideline
100 yards
CENTER LINE
The middle point of the pitch.
25-YARD LINE
DEFENDER'S MARK FOR CORNERS
The defenders can stand between these two lines when helping their goalkeeper defend a penalty corner.
ATTACKER'S MARK FOR CORNERS
This is where the first hit of the penalty corner is taken.

THE RULES

TIMING

A field hockey match is played in two halves. Each half is 35 minutes long. At the end of the second half, whichever team has the most goals wins. There are two umpires on the field making sure that players aren't breaking the rules.

PLAYER TAKING PENALTY

MISCONDUCT

Misconduct is when an umpire feels a player needs to be **SANCTIONED**. The umpire will show players a colored card; each card represents a certain amount of time during which the player will be suspended. This is the order the cards come in:

2-MINUTE SUSPENSION

5-MINUTE SUSPENSION

SUSPENSION FOR THE REST OF THE GAME

FREE HITS

IF A PLAYER DOES SOMETHING WRONG, THE OPPOSING TEAM WILL BE AWARDED A free hit.

If a violation is committed by a defender inside the quarter of the pitch nearest their goal, then a penalty corner will be awarded to the opposing team. If a defender commits a serious VIOLATION inside their shooting circle, a penalty stroke will be awarded to the opposing team.

WHAT NOT TO DO

Here are some things that you aren't allowed to do in field hockey. Don't:

- Use the curved side of the stick to hit the ball
- Shield the ball with your body or stick
- Charge, hit, or shove other players
- Move the ball with anything other than your stick
- Stop an opponent from using their stick in any way
- Make the ball rise into the air on purpose, unless making a shot in the shooting circle

THIS WOULD BE A FOUL BECAUSE THE PLAYERS ARE PURPOSELY BUMPING INTO EACH OTHER.

THE EVENTS

RECREATIONAL AND REGIONAL TEAMS

If you have a school team, or a team that plays **RECREATIONALLY**, and you want to start competing, there are lots of ways you can get involved. Ask a teacher, parent, or sports coach how to join a local league.

AMATEUR FIELD HOCKEY TEAM IN TRAINING

THE BIG LEAGUES

As field hockey players get better and better, they can start playing at higher levels. After regional games come national ones. This means you play teams from all over your country. Then comes playing internationally, which means playing for your country. There are lots of tournaments for different areas around the world, such as The Asian Championships, African Championships, European Championships, and the Pan American Championships.

IN MANY INTERNATIONAL TOURNAMENTS, COUNTRIES FROM THE SAME **CONTINENT** COMPETE AGAINST EACH OTHER.

WOMEN'S JUNIOR ASIAN CUP

WORLD TOURNAMENTS

There are many international field hockey competitions in which countries from all over the world compete against each other. Some of these include the Hockey World Cup and the Champions Trophy.

USA VS. ENGLAND IN THE 2014 HOCKEY WORLD CUP

THE OLYMPICS

One of the most **PRESTIGIOUS** world tournaments is the Olympics. Lots of countries compete in a variety of games, one of which is field hockey. Since women's field hockey became an official Olympic sport in 1980, the teams with the most gold medals are the Netherlands and Australia; both have won three times.

NETHERLANDS VS. SOUTH AFRICA, 2014 YOUTH OLYMPIC GAMES

THE ONES TO WATCH

There are some very talented field hockey players that are at the top of their game. Let's take a look at some of them!

MADDIE HINCH

FACT FILE:

Date of Birth: October 8, 1988

Country of Birth: Great Britain

Height: 5'6" (1.68 m)

Position: Goalkeeper

Hinch is an amazing goalkeeper. She was awarded the best goalkeeper award by the FIH in 2016 after saving four penalties in the Olympic finals, securing Great Britain the gold medal. Winning 11 medals in only eight years, Hinch is definitely worth watching.

JULIETA JANKUNAS

FACT FILE:

Date of Birth: January 20, 1999

Country of Birth: Argentina

Height: 5'6" (1.68 m)

Position: Forward

As a junior hockey player, Jankunas played for Argentina's national team at the 2014 Summer Youth Olympics where she helped her team win bronze. She now plays for the senior national team, and at 19 was the youngest player competing in the 2018 Women's Hockey World Cup.

PLAY LIKE A GIRL

PLAY LIKE A GIRL

LIDEWIJ WELTEN

FACT FILE:

Date of Birth: July 16, 1990

Country of Birth: Netherlands

Height: 5'7" (1.7 m)

Position: Forward

When Welten played for the Dutch youth national team, it was obvious that she was soon to be a star in the field hockey world. After winning two Olympic golds with the Dutch team in 2008 and 2012, and getting (another!) gold at the Women's Hockey World Cup in 2018, she has proven this prediction correct.

ALEX DANSON

FACT FILE:

Date of Birth: May 21, 1985

Country of Birth: Great Britain

Height: 5'5" (1.65 m)

Position: Forward

Scoring over 100 goals in international tournaments, it is unsurprising that Danson was appointed as Great Britain's captain. After letting Olympic gold slip through Britain's fingers in 2012, Danson came back with a vengeance in 2016 to win the Olympic gold. She has since been awarded an MBE for her contributions toward field hockey.

THE HALL

Field hockey has a history of amazing players. Let's take a look at the best of the best.

A great goal scorer, Natascha Keller was one of the best hockey players in the world. She could make an accurate shot from even the toughest of positions. Playing internationally for Germany, she competed in five Olympic Games and won gold in 2004. She was even awarded Player of the Year by the FIH in 1999.

Marsha Cox is a South African superstar with an amazing story. Her mother, Marian Marescia, was also a field hockey player. Although Cox's mother was a very good player, she was never allowed to play internationally for her country. This was because of apartheid. Cox followed in her mother's footsteps as a great player and has not only played for her country, but captained the team in many international tournaments.

APARTHEID WAS WHEN PEOPLE WERE SEPARATED BY RACE BECAUSE OF PREJUDICES.

OF FAME

If there's one thing we know about Maartje Pauman, it's that her arms must hurt from lifting all those trophies. Winning two Olympic golds, two World Championships, and three European Championships, she is considered one of the most internationally **DECORATED** field hockey players. She even managed to score 11 goals in the Beijing Olympics in 2008.

Luciana Aymar is regarded as one of the greatest female players of all time. With the nickname "La Maga" (The Magician), she is known for her devilish dribbling skills that she uses to get past any opponent. These talents and skills have led her to have been awarded Player of the Year an amazing eight times by the FIH.

THE FACTS AND STATS

PLAYERS CAN RUN UP TO 5 MILES (8 KM) DURING A SINGLE MATCH.

THE NETHERLANDS WOMEN'S TEAM HAVE WON THE MOST OLYMPIC MEDALS WITH THREE GOLDS, TWO SILVERS, AND THREE BRONZES.

FIELD HOCKEY IS THE NATIONAL SPORT OF PAKISTAN.

PAKISTAN AT THE ASIAN HOCKEY FEDERATION (AHF) WORLD CUP

AT THE 2012 LONDON OLYMPICS, FIELD HOCKEY WAS THE 3RD MOST **SPECTATED** SPORT.

ONLY RIGHT-HANDED STICKS ARE USED IN OFFICIAL MATCHES. THIS IS BECAUSE WHEN A RIGHT-HANDED STICK AND A LEFT-HANDED STICK ARE USED TOGETHER IT IS MORE LIKELY THAT PLAYERS WILL ACCIDENTALLY HIT EACH OTHER.

KATE RICHARDSON-WALSH IS GREAT BRITAIN'S MOST **CAPPED** FEMALE FIELD HOCKEY PLAYER IN THE COUNTRY'S HISTORY WITH OVER 370 APPEARANCES AND 13 YEARS AS CAPTAIN OF THE NATIONAL TEAM.

YOUR TEAM

If field hockey sounds like the sport for you, why not try to get a team together? Ask all your friends if they want to give it a go. If you have a gym or playing field in your school or where you live, why not try it?

If you can't find anything at your school, you could go to your local sports center to use the field and equipment there. If you and your friends enjoy the sport, keep practicing. The more you practice, the better you will get.

YOU NEVER KNOW, YOU MIGHT BE IN THE HALL OF FAME ONE DAY!

GLOSSARY

amateur	someone who does something for fun rather than professionally
breathable	something that lets air pass through it
capped	(in sports) this is the total number of times an athlete has appeared in international games
circumference	the length around the widest part of a ball
continent	a very large area of land that is often made up of many countries, such as Africa or Europe
decorated	in a profession, this is when a person has have been given awards, medals, or trophies for their work
essential	something that is important and necessary
FIH	Fédération Internationale de Hockey, the official organization that makes decisions about field hockey
MBE	Member of the British Empire, an award given for an outstanding achievement or service to the community
opposing	on the team playing against you
prejudices	opinions, judgments, or beliefs that are formed without taking the facts into account
prestigious	an important and highly regarded status
recreationally	to do something for fun rather than professionally
reflexes	reactions to something that you do without thinking
sanctioned	threatened or penalized for not following the rules
spectated	viewed or watched
sprint	to run as fast as you can
surface area	the total amount of surface an object has
suspension	the act of being removed from the game for a time
synthetic	man-made and not found in nature
versatile	able to be adapted in order to fit many different functions or activities
violation	a breaking of the rules

INDEX